HOW WRITE OFF YOUR PAIN?

HOW TO WRITE OFF YOUR PAIN?

Dr. Ridwana Sanam

Gullybaba Publishing House Pvt. Ltd.
ISO 9001 & ISO 14001 CERTIFIED CO.

PUBLICATION

Published under the faithful principles of

Gullybaba Publishing House Pvt. Ltd.

Regd. Office: 2525/193, 1st Floor, Onkar Nagar-A,
Tri Nagar, Delhi-110035,
Ph.: 09350849407, 09312235086
Branch Office: 1A/2A, 20, Hari Sadan, Ansari Road,
Daryaganj, New Delhi-110002, **Ph.:** 011-23239034, 011-45794768

First Edition: 2018

ISBN:978-93-86276-92-6

© Publishing and Reprint rights reserved with the Publisher. No part of this publication may be reproduced, distributed or transmitted in any form or by any means, including photocopying, recording or other electronic or mechanical methods, without the prior written permission of the publisher.

Disclaimer: Publisher disclaims any proprietary or personality rights in and relating to the images. Images and representation in the work are purely informational and their use in the work does not, in any manner, amount to any endorsement or association with the person, place or organisation as such. Further the contents of the title are informational sake and in no manner, whatsoever, shall be considered as a treatment by any medical professional or practitioner or any form of medical prescription, diagnosis or any similar activity.

Layout Design: Gullybaba Publishing House Pvt. Ltd.

Dedication

*I am dedicating this book to
my younger brother*
**Mohd. Yusuf
Kayte**, *who is always
in my heart and prayers.*

Contents

Foreword	*ix*
Preface	*xi*
Acknowledgements	*xiii*
About the Author	*xv*
Why this Book?	*xvii*
How to Use this Book?	*xix*
1. Conception of the Book	1
2. Prevention Management	9
3. Repetitive Stress Injury (RSI)	13
4. Correct Posture	21
5. Neck Pain	35

6.	Back Pain	45
7.	Knee, Foot and Shoulder Pain	53
8.	Arthritis	57
9.	Prevention During Pregnancy	85
10.	Role of Diet	89
11.	Lifestyle Modifications	97
12.	Good Posture Goodies	103
13.	Easy Tips and Tricks to Remember	117
14.	Summary and Conclusion	131

Foreword

I have had the privilege of knowing Dr. Sanam since 2012, and it gives me great pleasure to see her writing this book, which will serve as an important guide for patients. I first became acquainted with KRV and Dr. Sanam when I injured my elbow. I was already familiar with KRV, as my sister had undergone treatment there for a serious back injury in 2011, after which she was able to resume her normal physical activity. This gave me great confidence, and I consulted with Dr. Sanam during the summer of 2012, and started my treatment, which subsequently resolved my issue. Unfortunately, I injured my left shoulder in 2014, and returned to KRV once again, and I could return to full physical activity following treatment, and a regular exercise regimen prescribed by Dr. Sanam and her team.

Dr. Sanam has extensive practical experience as a practising physiotherapist, and has treated many patients successfully, since establishing her clinical practice in 2007. Having seen many patients with a variety of symptoms, she became interested in the subject of prevention of injuries. During the time, I was being treated by Dr. Sanam, I became familiar with her passion for preventative measures to avoid injuries, and her desire to teach others about this subject. I truly admired her selflessness as a clinician, who was investing her own time to keep patients healthy, so that they would not need to be treated. Over the course of time, I realised that keeping patients healthy is her life mission.

This book is inspired by her personal passion of being able to help people keep healthy through simple preventative measures. In this book, she has explained techniques in layman terms, which can be used as a practical self-help guide not only for those that have been living with pain, but also for the people who are interested in living a lifestyle free of pain.

After having read the book, I can say with utmost confidence that this book will serve as an extremely helpful guide in the prevention and management of pain.

Vishal Wanchoo

(President & CEO, General Electric, South Asia)

Preface

As a physiotherapist, I have dedicated my college education and entire professional life to the healing of patients in pain. Since I started my clinical practice in 2007, I discovered that it is my personal passion to be able to cure pain, and it gives me immense satisfaction to see that patients can live pain-free lives once again. During the many years of treating patients, I recognised the equal importance of preventing injuries and became interested in this aspect of the medical profession. I was convinced that being able to educate patients on prevention and physiotherapy, would pave the way for a healthy future for them. I also recognised that the best way to broadly propagate knowledge on this subject, could be a book that would be able to be easily understood. Many of my patients over the years encouraged me to write a book on this subject that could help them and others.

Given that our health is extremely precious and never to be taken for granted, we must evaluate our lifestyle choices. The health choices that we make today will not only affect us in the present, but more importantly pave the way for our future well-being. As a Physiotherapist (Manual Practitioner), I strongly believe that maintaining correct alignment of one's body, posture, diet and exercise is essential to the prevention of injuries, and is an investment in protecting our most valuable resource — our health.

The book is written so that it can be used as a self-help guide with step-by-step guidance for understanding the basics of one's body, techniques for prevention of injuries, and when to seek help in the event of an injury. I have explained facts in layman terms, and am confident that following the guidelines will help people preventing and curing pain. I am dedicating this book to you to make your life pain free.

Dr. Ridwana Sanam

Acknowledgements

First and foremost, I would like to thank my **parents**, who gave me abundant love and provided a nurturing environment during my early childhood years, which enabled me to grow up as independent and self-confident.

I also want to thank **Dr. Mala Arora and Dr. Narender Pal** for introducing and teaching me about Repetitive Stress Injury (RSI), and for their ongoing guidance and support.

I would also like to thank **Mrs. Meenu Ghosh** and **Mr. Sandip Ghosh,** who have always motivated me to do my very best.

I want to especially thank all **my patients**, the **KRV Physiotherapy team**, for their suggestions, feedback, and encouragement to publish a book that could be helpful for everyone.

I also want to thank **my brothers and sisters** for always being there for me. I would also like to thank **Mr. Vishal Wanchoo** for his guidance and well-crafted foreword.

I am thankful to **Mr. Dinesh Verma**, MD, Gullybaba Publishing House and his team for their support and suggestions throughout the creative process.

About the Author

Dr. Ridwana Sanam is a leading Consultant Physiotherapist and Woman Entrepreneur, well known for her work in the field of Clinical Physiotherapy and Education. She has done short term courses like Kineseo-Taping (Japan), Band & Ball (UK), Manual Therapy (Singapore) and Dry Needling (AIIMS, India).

She founded KRV in 2007 and incorporated KVR Healthcare and Physiotherapy Pvt. Ltd. in 2011. She has over 10 years of clinical experience, having treated lacs of patients across India, as well as from neighbouring countries in South Asia and Middle East.

She is well versed in the latest technology and techniques in physiotherapy, and through her direct treatment of patients over the last 10 years, she has prevented more than 50,000 surgeries of Osteoarthritis, Slip Disc and ACL Tear. In addition to committing herself to the effective diagnosis and treatment of injuries, she is also a firm believer in the prevention of injuries by adopting simple techniques for an ergonomic and healthy lifestyle. She developed this interest having treated many patients, where injuries were preventable and this inspired her to contribute her knowledge by writing this book, a practical and simple guide for the prevention of musculoskeletal Repetitive Stress Injuries (RSI).

Dr. Ridwana Sanam has received numerous recognitions and awards for her work in Clinical Practice and Education: Crowned as Angel in Medical Services in 2013, Best Physiotherapist in India by brand icon and renowned actress and fitness model Shilpa Shetty in 2017, World Women Leadership Congress Awards for the Best Entrepreneurial Skills, 10th National Women Excellence Award in 2017, and Best Physiotherapy Consultant by Professional Golfers' Association.

Why this Book?

As a doctor, my relationship with my patients is more than a fiduciary one. My patients deserve the very best treatment and a healthy life. If I fail to live up to their expectations, I feel that the purpose of my life will remain unfulfilled.

While treating my patients, I developed the desire of writing a book on physiotherapy. I wanted to ensure that any patient, independent of whether they were my patient, deserve a good education in physiotherapy because the proper education in this field will pave the way for a healthy future.

Physiotherapy, also referred to as 'physical therapy', involves evaluating, diagnosing and treating a range of diseases, disorders and disabilities using physical means. Practised by physiotherapists or physical therapists, physiotherapy is considered within the realm of conventional medicine. The very purpose of writing this book is to educate my readers about what physiotherapy means, which areas of body pain can be healed with physiotherapy, what physiotherapists do in treatment, and other relevant topics.

I encourage you to read every chapter and try the exercises which are relevant to your problem. Also learn how to do things correctly, as the right movements will achieve the desired outcomes.

How to Use this Book?

This book is in your hands because you have good reason to believe that by reading this book, you will be able to alleviate your pain to a large extent. And the purpose of writing this book is to live up to that expectation.

Before you start reading the book, I would like to give you some tips regarding the better use of this book:

- **Read the book in sequence:** I have seen readers thumbing through the pages, concentrating on a few topics. They choose to read only those topics or chapters that are related to themselves or their dear ones; however it is important to read the entire book in sequence. Reading it in this fashion will provide you with a comprehensive view of the subject matter and all the salient facts about physiotherapy.

- **Focus your attention on prevention management:** The chapter 'Prevention Management' enables you to understand the importance of prevention, and how it can help you to lead a pain-free life. You will be able to learn how to make small changes in day-to-day activities that can help prevent the development of future disorders.

- **Repetitive Stress Injury (RSI) needs a thorough review:** RSI is an integral part of physiotherapy. If you are a regular computer user, this content assumes even more importance for you. This chapter focuses on the various factors that cause Repetitive Stress Injury and how it can be prevented.

- **Special emphasis on sitting postures:** Correct posture is extremely important, most often not understood, and very easily correctable. This chapter focuses on the correct posture during various common activities performed by most of us, such as sitting while doing your work, reading a newspaper, eating your meal, etc. The chapter is written in a way that is very easy to understand, and by reading it, you should be able to educate others on "what should be your correct posture?"

- **Conclusion:** By reading all the chapters, you may feel like you need not read the 'conclusion', however don't make the mistake of omitting it. The conclusion carries all the essentials of physiotherapy that we have discussed, things to be taken into consideration, and practised daily.

I am very optimistic that the above-mentioned suggestions will help you extract the maximum value out of this book.

1
CONCEPTION OF THE BOOK

The book is written primarily for the people who have been living with pain for years, and for those who have experienced pain and want to prevent its reoccurrence. Pain is nothing to be scared about; it is just a body signal hinting at underlying pathology.

This book is about understanding the body signals in the musculoskeletal system and preventing pathological disorders.

Before I start the explanation about the bone system, or in medical terminology 'the musculoskeletal system', I would like to share an incident that touched my heart and inspired me to write this book.

When I was at KRV Clinic, Faridabad, a girl came to me on 14th March, 2007 with her mother. This young and simple girl used to work at a renowned multinational company, at a call centre in Gurugram. She was fired from the company, as she was suffering from facial palsy. 'Facial palsy' is a condition in which one side of the facial muscles becomes paralyzed. She did not have any financial backup, as she had lost her father. She had little hope, as her condition had already led to losing her JOB! Tired of meeting countless physicians, ENT/orthopaedic surgeons/neurosurgeons, she finally did some research on the Internet, and found out about physiotherapy treatment available for her condition. Sad and depressed, she came to me as her last resort. I had a very strange and unexplained feeling when she said with tears in her eyes, that she had no money to pay for the treatment. I had treated many patients, but never had a patient walking into my clinic and asking for treatment, but not being able to pay. The helplessness in her eyes made me believe in what she said and made me very curious to know the root cause of her problem. I thought that her condition was easily treatable, and hence I asked her to narrate her full story. Here is what she said:

"I had neck pain for which I was referred to the company's physician. As there were no significant findings, the company's physician referred me to an ENT specialist as I had headaches, earaches, along with neck pain. The reports did not indicate any problems, and so the ENT specialist prescribed painkillers, but they didn't help me at all. After a few days, I started developing giddiness and nausea, for which I went to see a neurosurgeon. He said I had vertigo and prescribed medication for it. There was no improvement in my condition with this course of treatment, so I consulted an orthopaedic surgeon. He assured me that my symptoms were due to stress, and psychological pain, as the reports of the x-rays and MRI did not reveal any problem. He advised me to take more painkillers, apply analgesic ointment with hot fomentation, and rest for a few days. I kept following the doctor's recommendation, with the hope of getting well. But, one morning when I woke up, I noticed that I had facial asymmetry. I was shocked, sad, and angry at the same time, as I just couldn't get an accurate diagnosis and treatment. I am very depressed as my illness cost me my job; the company no longer wanted me to work as they said I'm not fit for the job."

I calmly listened to the girl's story and then started her examination. On her assessment, I noticed acute 'trapezitis'.

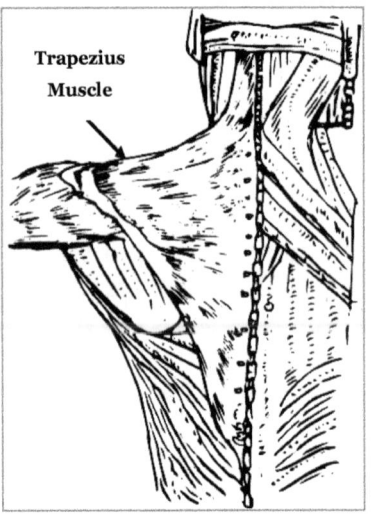

Trapezius is a big muscle of upper back which stretches from neck to mid back.

Her neck was tilted to one side. She not only had facial palsy, but also had a lot of inflammation and muscle spasm, or tightness around her neck. I started treating her for neck pain and facial palsy. While treating her neck, I also diagnosed misalignment of the upper two neck bones. Sometimes, working long hours with the wrong posture creates an imbalance of the head over the spine, which places pressure on the nerves, and can cause muscle tightness or spasms. With the treatment, and as her muscle spasm decreased, she started showing improvement in her facial muscles as well. Later, I started facial muscle stimulation, which helped her recover even faster. The treatment not only recovered her facial palsy completely, but also her self- confidence. She is now fully recovered and has started working in a new company.

This whole incident made me realise the importance of awareness. The girl lost her job and the company lost an employee. The company can hire a new employee, but is there any guarantee that the recruit won't suffer from any illness? Removing employee may not be the solution, but to remove the cause certainly is.

The whole idea of this book is to understand 'Prevention Management'. Why can't we educate people about prevention and help them understand the 'First Signal' and seek the right treatment immediately, before it becomes a disorder? This book will certainly help educate people about the basics of one's body and whom to approach when they have any musculoskeletal problems. For the bone and muscle system, there is no need to consult a physician. Patients trust physicians, but physicians cannot detect early stage problems of bone alignment, joint, muscle, nerve, and ligament issues, as x-rays and MRI will not reveal a clinical finding. A knowledgeable and experienced physiotherapist can help with conservative treatment for the bone and muscle system, however, if there is no improvement within a week, consulting with an orthopaedic specialist is advisable.

> *It is recommended that companies enrol physiotherapists along with physicians for early prevention management.*

It is recommended that companies enrol physiotherapists along with physicians for early prevention management.

In today's highly competitive scenario, it is imperative for companies to increase productivity, which consequently puts immense pressure on the employees to perform and deliver. This in turn often results in long and stressful working hours. Health issues invariably arise, resulting in sick leave and loss of productivity. Early prevention facilities would go a long way in increasing productivity and maintaining good health and fitness. The solution to the problem cannot be achieved by simply changing furniture, but by implementing few simple lifestyle changes. This will lead to manifold benefits in maintaining fitness.

2

PREVENTION MANAGEMENT

The motto of my book is to spread awareness to the common people, and make them understand the importance of prevention.

> *Prevention is just a conscious effort undertaken while performing daily activities that can prevent a condition (bone-joint system) from occurring.*

PREVENTION MANAGEMENT

Did it ever occur to you that the cause of the pain in your hip travelling towards the back of your leg could have been prevented by just changing the placement of your wallet away from your back pocket? Try this and I am sure you will see an improvement. This simple change could prevent sciatica and other health problems.

Men/Women have become machines today. We work 24×7, and I understand that even if I say that you must rest, you cannot. Bringing small changes in daily activities, or as I call them adaptations in your life, can prevent the development of disorders.

Unfortunately, when people come to me, they have already developed pathology. When I explain to them the do's and don'ts of daily activities, they tell me "I wish I knew of these prevention techniques before." But, it's never too late!

> *Postural correction and lifestyle modification started at any point can do wonders.*

It prevents you from developing disease, and if you already have a problem, it helps in correcting it. I often hear from my patients, "had I known about these preventive measures, I would have been in a better position to cure my disorder."

I always tell them to concentrate on their posture, posture of their children, eating habits, walking and sitting style, their shoes, and the way they carry their bags. It only requires a keen eye, and good observation. Prevention should start during the childhood years itself. There are numerous musculoskeletal deformities that can be prevented by just taking proper postures and lifestyle changes into consideration.

In this book, I want to make people aware of Occupational Overuse Syndrome, Prevention Management, and a few small tips, which could make their life easier.

Many people that I interact with, share with me, that they remain seated in the office, have maids at home for help, and hence they hardly do any physical work in their office, at home, or outside. They always wonder then, how can they possibly suffer? Well, it is not what you do; it is rather how you do it, that really causes an overuse syndrome, or repetitive stress syndrome.

3
REPETITIVE STRESS INJURY

Repetitive Stress Injury (RSI) is a term for a number of specific injuries caused by the repetitive movement of any particular part of the body. Specifically, RSI is known as an 'Occupational Overuse Syndrome' that affects nerves, tendons and muscles.

For example, you get up in the morning, do your daily activities, get ready for the office, drive to the office, work in front of a computer for hours at a stretch, drive back home, eat and sleep. I am sure this has been the daily routine of most of my readers for years. It's an everyday job; you follow a similar daily schedule. But you forget that this daily repetitive pattern is what is causing repetitive stress on your joints, bones, muscles and ligaments. If you are not aware of the right posture and biomechanics, you injure yourself while performing daily activities. The activities can be just getting up from bed, to working on a computer, or prolonged periods of sitting. There is an important reason for covering this topic, as most of the time patients tell me that they did not do any activity that could have caused exertion, however pain just started suddenly. But, the reason for the pain is that the daily stress to your joints has finally reached a threshold, and now the body is giving a signal to an underlying pathology through pain.

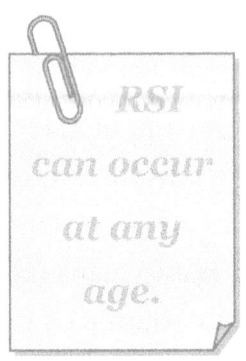

RSI can occur at any age.

The causes of RSI can be broadly classified into:

- Repetition — repeated motions of a body part
- Awkward Posture — maintaining awkward body positions
- Static Posture — holding parts of the body in one position for a long time

Have you pictured yourself while working? Try to visualise yourself and recollect—are you leaning forward on the desk, sitting without a back support, neck rotated to one side? Have you ever noticed your child studying sitting on the bed, without any back support, bending too far forward to write or read a book, carrying heavy bags on one shoulder, men or women standing in the kitchen and cooking for hours at a stretch? If you think carefully, you will realise that you tend to keep your body in very awkward postures for too long, or static, which causes stress on your bone and joint-system.

RSI results from the repetitive typical tasks that you perform such as excessive use of computer and flat-light touch keyboards that permit high-speed typing have resulted in an epidemic of injuries of the hands, arms and shoulders. Another name for the condition is 'Cumulative Trauma Disorder'. The reason it is called 'cumulative' is because the initial overuse injury leads to the next overuse injury, and hence there is a compounding effect to these types of injuries. Long hours of study, prolonged sitting in lecture rooms, carrying heavy bags, excessive use of mobiles, increased use of computers or laptops, incorrect diet habits, wearing improper shoes, etc., and other reasons like continuous pressure of performance, competition, choice of correct career, and family stress lead to increase chances of developing RSI. It is assumed that a large percentage of the population is suffering from RSI.

Types of Repetitive Stress Injury (RSI)

'Repetitive Stress Injury' is a broad term which includes micro trauma at various joints. It can affect your neck, shoulder, back or legs. Medically, the conditions are listed below:

- Neck Pain/Trapezitis
- Shoulder Pain

- Bursitis
- Epicondylitis
- Carpal Tunnel Syndrome
- Trigger Finger
- Tenosynovitis
- Mechanical/Postural Back Pain, Knee Pain
- The early sign of RSI is pain and inflammation. If you have these signs, you must go to a physical therapist for treatment. Treatment at an early stage is important to prevent further damage.

Negligence

Neglecting the early signals can cause the postural problems to turn into structural disorders. Results of negligence are:

- Cervical Spondylosis
- Secondary Postural Changes (Scoliosis/Kyphosis)
- Lumbar Spondylosis
- Piriformis Syndrome
- Degenerative Disc Disease

- Knee Osteoarthritis
- Calcaneal Spurs/Plantar Fasciitis
- Varicose Veins

Symptoms

Symptoms of RSI can range from mild to severe. It develops gradually and worsens with time. Some common symptoms are:

- Pain
- Swelling, inflammation
- Numbness or tingling sensation
- Decreased movement of a joint
- Stiffness of body part(s)

Prevention

We all know that 'prevention is better than cure'. We've heard this saying so many times. But what exactly does it mean? Prevention is just a conscious effort undertaken while performing daily activities that can prevent a disorder or disease.

RSI prevention is all about postural correction, ergonomics, recognising the body's health status, lifestyle modification and healthy living.

> *Prevention begins from childhood. There are so many musculoskeletal deformities that can be prevented if proper care and precaution is exercised during childhood years.*

The most common condition that can be detected at childhood is 'flat foot'. Early detection cannot only correct the defect, but also prevent early arthritis which can occur because of flat foot. Once flat foot is detected, medial insoles should be used. Some basic exercises of the feet can work wonders and develop the medial arch.

Some common preventative measures are discussed below:

- Teaching children to sit in a proper posture can prevent spinal deformities like 'scoliosis', in which the body is tilted to one side. Carrying heavy school bags on one side, or one shoulder, or even carrying heavy bags for too long, can affect the spinal posture.

- The spinal deformities like 'scoliosis', 'kyphosis' and excessive 'lordosis' can be prevented by not ignoring the first signal of the body which is a muscle spasm. Muscle spasms should be treated immediately.

- The use of moist hot towels on the back, anti-inflammatory ointment is a very simple, and the most effective treatment for muscle spasms.

- Once the muscle spasm subsides, the back alignment gets automatically corrected.

4
CORRECT POSTURE

Correct posture involves training your body to stand, walk, sit and lie in positions where the least strain is placed on supporting muscles and ligaments, during movement or weight-bearing activities.

Sitting Posture

Correct sitting posture is extremely important. The most common incorrect sitting postures frequently practised by people in the office during long working hours, are shown below.

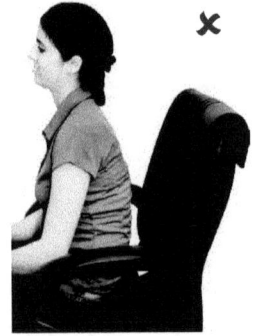

Incorrect Sitting Postures

Chair Curvature with Soft Arm Support

There are various ergonomic chairs available in the market, however selecting the best one for you is very important.

The back of the chair should be curved in the shape of your spine. Our back is not straight, it's curved. Therefore, straight back chairs are not good for your back. It should also have height adjustment levers. Many people complain that the office management is not providing them the right chair. While it is important to have the right type of chair, it is equally important to know the right way to sit.

- Your lower back should always be supported. You can keep a small cushion behind your lower back for support.

- The height of your working table and chair should be such that when you sit, your elbows should bend at 90 degrees.

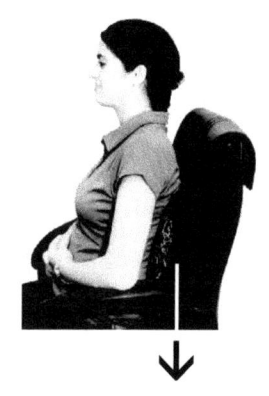

Soft pillow between back and chair

- The chair should have soft armrests. Soft armrests at the correct height are very important.

- In my practice, I have noticed 80 per cent of the people complaining of neck and shoulder pain, because their arms are not supported, during prolonged working hours on a computer.

- When you work for too long at the desk without your elbows supported on the armrest, stress develops on the muscles and nerves of the neck and shoulder, leading to neck and shoulder pain.

The easiest way of preventing this is by supporting your elbows on the armrest.

- If you don't have an armrest then you can pull your chair close to the table, and keep your elbows supported on the table. The computer screen should be exactly in front of you, at a height of your face, to avoid unnecessary neck bending and neck rotations.

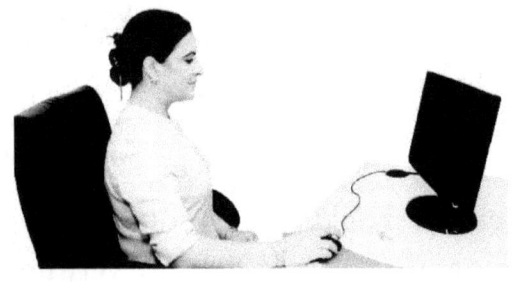

- Correct typing technique and postures are of prime importance.

The right equipment setup, and good work habits are much more important for prevention, than ergonomic gadgets like split keyboards or palm rests.

Don't Pound on the Keys

- While typing, keep your wrist supported. Hold the mouse lightly, don't grip it hard or squeeze it.

- Wrists also should not be bent to the side. It is better to learn and use keyboard equivalent commands.

Don't Strain your Eyes

- Increase your font size; this will put less strain on your eyes, as well as on your neck. If you write in small fonts, you will unnecessarily bend your neck to read.

Carrying a Laptop Bag

- Do not carry your laptop on one side, or one shoulder. This will create muscle imbalance, and strain your neck and shoulder. The best way to carry your laptop is in a backpack.

Relaxing

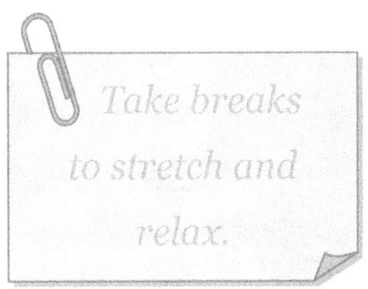

Take breaks to stretch and relax.

This means both — momentary breaks every few minutes and longer breaks every hour. I understand that while working, you get so involved that you absolutely forget to take a break. Small breaks work like a power booster and prepare your body to work more.

- Stretch your arms, look up at the ceiling, stretch the neck, stand, take a stroll, have a cup of tea and rejuvenate yourself.

You will be surprised to see the changes that these small breaks bring to your fitness.

- Some common stretches that can be practised while seated in the office to help your posture:

  (i) **Shoulder Bracing:** Place your hands on the thigh, pull your shoulders back. Hold the position for 5-10 sec. and relax. Repeat 5-10 times.

  (ii) **Triceps Stretch:** Bend your elbow 180 degrees, and place your hand behind your shoulder. Hold the elbow with other hand, and push the arm back to apply the stretch. Hold the position for 5-10 sec. and relax. Repeat 3 times. Repeat the same stretch on the other side.

  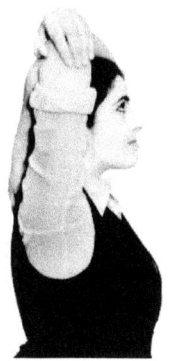

Clasp your hands and place them on your head, then stretch them upwards as shown in the picture below.

Similarly, clasp your hands, bring them in front of your chest and then stretch as shown in the picture below.

Use of Cell Phone

> Don't tuck cell phone between your shoulder and ear.

- Try to talk less on the telephone or cell phone. If your profession demands long telephonic conversation use head phones instead.

Incorrect Way

- We see so many people around us driving a car and talking on the phone at the same time. When you talk on the phone you usually bend and rotate your neck to one side. Also, your arm is unsupported. This puts undue pressure on your muscles and nerves.

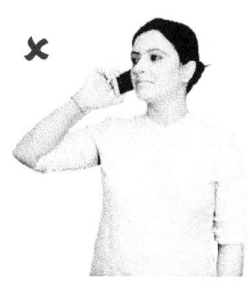

Incorrect Way

CORRECT POSTURE

- Keep your elbow close to your body, don't keep it unsupported. Keeping the hand close to the body will provide support and prevent fatigue in your arm as well as in the neck.

Correct Way

Too much use of phone for texting or playing games leads to pain in the wrist and thumbs.

When we are texting or playing games, we tend to bend our neck too much for very long, which causes neck pain and eventually RSI.

Incorrect Way

Therefore, it is very important that while texting, you hold your mobile device higher (approximately at your eye level) to avoid unnecessary bending of the neck.

Correct Way

Footwear

I want to mention one very important point here, which plays an important part in maintaining a good posture. We put in so much effort to look good, wear the best of clothes, but tend to be negligent of our feet.

Selecting the right shoes helps prevent RSI to a large extent.

Give Comfort to your Feet

- Wear soft soles. Wearing soft soles can prevent heel pain, knee pain and even back pain. In today's fashion world, lots of options are available, from high-heel shoes to flip flops. But the sole of the shoe is the most essential point to be kept in mind.

- High-heeled shoes put more pressure on the forefoot, which frequently leads to back pain. It affects the knee muscles which causes difficulty in maintaining your balance.

- Prolonged use of high heels can lead to osteoarthritis. High heels can also lead to deformities like hammer toes, bunions, neuronal and bunionettes.

- Walking in high heels shifts your centre of gravity, putting undue stress on your joints and back. A heel height of 1.5 inches is optimal, and women can wear them for daily use but it is important to have soft supporting soles.

- Flats, slippers, or flip flops on the other hand cause lower back and ankle pain due to the 'clopping' gait that they encourage. They often cause blisters, create serious arch problems over time and make it painful to walk.

- Plantar fasciitis is a very common condition which occurs due to wearing hard flat slippers. Plantar fasciitis is a condition where there is inflammation of the fascia or sole.

- If the footwear is not changed, the condition worsens and ultimately medical or surgical intervention is required to correct the problem.

Support the Arms

- Put your hands in your pockets, or clasped behind your back, also referred to as the "military posture".

- Put your hands on your thigh or table, in case you have a chair without an armrest.

- If you have a habit of sitting cross-legged, do switch to alternate legs

every 3-5 min. This will prevent an over stretch on one side. Side with cross-leg is a good way to stretch your thigh (hip) muscles. Avoid sitting cross-legged if you have pain.

Sleeping Right

- Do turn to one side while getting up from the bed.

Postural Realignment

If you have long working hours and you are not able to maintain the right posture, I advise you to wear a

simple brace. I'm not saying that it is mandatory to wear the brace, nor am I promoting it, but, I am recommending this as an option for those people who find it hard to maintain their posture.

5

NECK PAIN

Neck pain is the most common problem affecting people in any age group. Patients who come and see me often ask, "Doctor, am I suffering from cervical spondylitis?" Well, at the age of 20, you cannot have spondylitis, it's RSI or Overuse Syndrome, which if left unattended, can advance to slip disc (prolapsed inter-vertebral disc).

Remember the Do's and Don'ts which can prevent the progression of this condition.

Do's for Neck Pain

- Most important Do's (things you should do) to prevent aggravating neck pain are as listed below:

- Turn to one side of the bed while getting up from the bed (right side or left side).

Step 1 Step 2

- Get up from the unaffected side (pain-free side).
- While sleeping, keep a rolled towel under the neck while lying on the back.

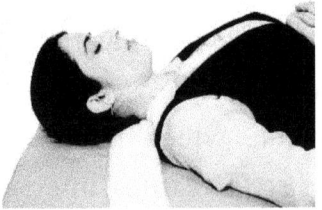

- Sleeping on your stomach is the best way of relaxing the back, and decompressing the nervous system.

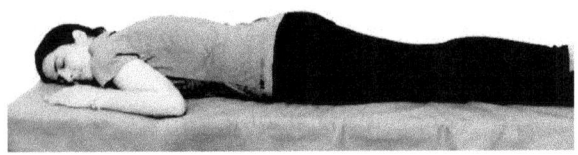

- If you cannot sleep on your stomach, lie on one side or half prone position.

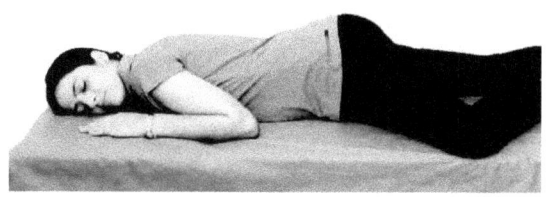

- **Thickness of the pillow:** There are no standard measurements in this regard. It varies from person to person. The best way to decide the thickness is to measure the distance between the base of the neck and tip of the shoulder.

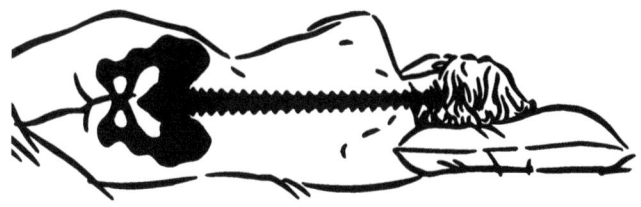

Very Important for Neck Pain

- Arms should be supported in one of the three positions:
    - **(i)** Hands in pockets
    - **(ii)** Hands on thighs or on table
    - **(iii)** Hand behind the back with elbows straight

> *Hanging hands puts additional stretch on the neck muscles (trapezius) due to gravity.*

- Avoid holding your head in one position. In order to avoid holding the head in the same position for long periods, take a break while working on a computer, driving or watching TV.

- Use a seat belt when in a car. Wearing a seat belt not only provides safety, but also stability as you sit in the car.

- Use a cervical collar if you have any giddiness associated with neck pain.

- Move shoulders backward (retraction of shoulders) every hour.

- While working during the day, most people keep sitting in a slouched position even if they know the importance of the right posture. Therefore, it is important to take periodic breaks and do some stretches.

Don'ts for Neck Pain

As I said, what not to do is more important. Listed below are the things, which should be avoided absolutely:

- Don't sleep straight on your back as it puts pressure on the spine.
- Don't bend your neck as it places undue stretch on the deep neck muscles.
- Avoid hanging of the arms as it stretches the trapezius muscle.
- Avoid sitting for prolonged time in stressful postures.
- Don't lift heavy weight on head or back.
- Don't drive for long hours. Take breaks.
- Avoid holding the telephone on one shoulder and leaning to one side for a long time.
- When you talk on the phone, don't turn your face to one side and bend your head towards the shoulder. This position stretches the neck muscles. Also, holding a phone in an unsupported hand places stress on the shoulder

and neck muscles. Use headphones if your profession requires long interactions.

- Don't put too many pillows below the neck and shoulder while sleeping.
- When you turn around, do not twist your neck or the body; instead turn around by moving your feet first, and bringing your entire body around.
- Don't use a hot water bottle on the neck as it can put undue pressure on it.
- Protracted pain may cause spasm in muscles and pressure over such muscle may irritate the muscle further and affect the nerves as well. Sometimes this can even cause radiating pain.

Shower Time and Care for the Neck

Keeping small things in mind while taking a shower can help to prevent neck pain.

- Use a shower if available, instead of using a mug and bucket, or a tap.

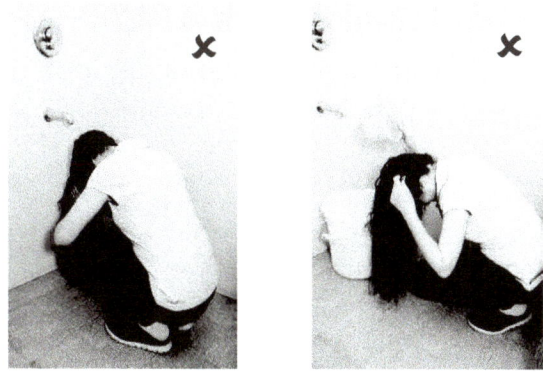

Incorrect Ways

- Don't face the shower. Your back should be towards the shower so that you don't need to bend your neck. Especially, while washing hair.

Correct Way

- Don't bend your neck and back while drying your hair with a towel.

Incorrect Ways

- Hold your hair to one side while drying. If you have short hair then stand straight, look upwards and dry your hair.

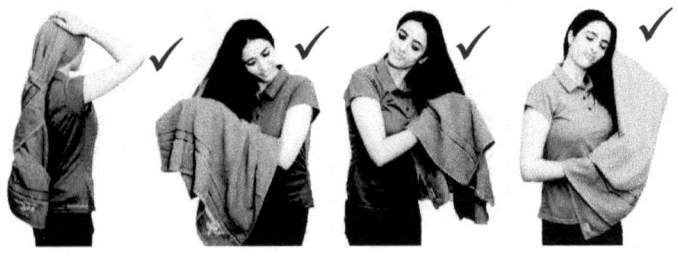

Correct Ways of Drying Hair

> The important point is that you should avoid bending the neck.

Advantages of a Hot Towel

- A hot towel covers a larger area (the entire upper back and neck). Moist heat is very effective in treating muscle spasms.

- A hot towel also opens the pores of the skin. Application of any pain relief ointment after moist heat will lead to good absorption. While sleeping, use a towel rolled under your neck while lying on your back, and a pillow of normal thickness inside lying position.

Sleeping on your stomach (prone lying) is the best way of sleeping, as I have covered in the previous chapter.

Neck Isometrics

Neck isometrics are basic neck muscle exercises, in which the muscle contracts without producing any neck movement. This exercise can be taught by a physiotherapist. When you visit a physiotherapist, he/she can explain the right technique, as any incorrect exercise can increase the pain.

Isometric Exercises for Neck

Isometric exercises are the safest ways to strengthen the neck muscles.

Benefits of Isometric Exercises

There are numerous benefits of implementing isometrics in the exercise:

- Muscle activation
- Muscle rehabilitation
- Muscle strengthening
- Increase flexibility

6

BACK PAIN

Wearing back support belts for an extended amount of time will cause muscle weakness. But, in acute cases, belts provide stability and should therefore be used.

Do's and Don'ts for Low Back Pain

Do's

- Please wear a lumbar belt. Wearing back support belts for a long time weakens the muscles. But, in severe cases, belts provide stability and should therefore be used.

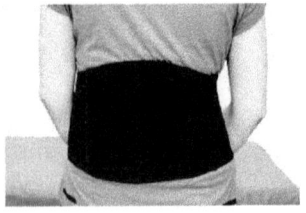

- As I have mentioned earlier, sleeping on your stomach is the best way of relaxing the spine, and keeping a pillow under the feet relaxes the legs. If sleeping on your stomach is not comfortable, and you sleep on your back, then place a towel under your neck and back and a pillow under the knees.

- Place a pillow under your knees, it provides relaxation to the leg muscles.

Variations in Sleeping Postures

- If you are unable to sleep on your stomach due to either chest breathlessness or heart problems, then opt for a position lying on your side, as shown in the picture.

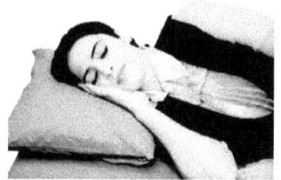

- Turn to one side of the bed while getting up from the bed (right side or left side).

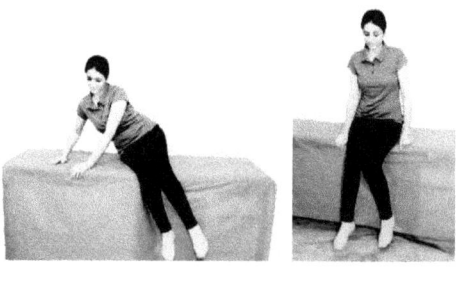

Step 1   Step 2

- Place a pillow between both the legs. This will prevent overstretching the upper leg muscles. It is a very comfortable position for sleeping. A pillow under the head is optional and depends on the comfort level.

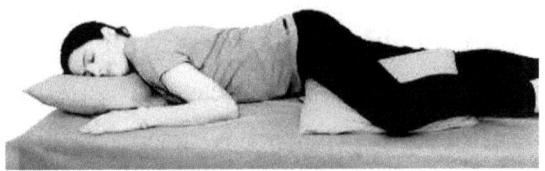

Older patients should avoid lying on the stomach as this can cause difficulty with breathing.

Soft cushioned pillow to support lower back

- Sit with your back straight, especially while sitting in the car.

- Ensure that your work-desk is at the correct and comfortable height. Your chair should have a back support and armrest.

- If your chair does not have an armrest, then pull your chair close to the desk and support your elbows on it.

- Always keep your knees and hips at the same level while sitting. Placing your knees above your hip level will disrupt the normal curvature of your back and give you the ache you would not want.

- Sit only for short intervals of time.

- If you are driving for a long time, try to take pit stops as often as possible. Get out of the car, stretch and walk around. This will give your back a well-deserved rest.

- Use a footstool when standing for a prolonged duration.

- For example, working in a kitchen, taking lecture at a seminar or a workshop, or in a classroom.

Don'ts

- Don't sit on soft couches. That will not enable you to sit straight.

- Don't slouch, as this will make your back curl and exert your lower back.
- While getting up, do not bend forward at your hip. Move ahead in your seat, apply pressure on your legs, straighten them, and then stand up.
- While lifting, stand as close to the object as possible, bend only at the knees while keeping your back straight.

Correct Ways of Lifting Objects

- Avoid lifting heavy objects as much as possible, as weightlifting puts additional stress on the back especially during back pain.

- Keep your back straight while mopping, using the vacuum cleaner, working with a lawn mower, etc.

Be Very Careful while Having Back Pain

- Don't jerk while lifting anything.

- Bending forward to lift anything should be strictly avoided as it increases the pressure on the spine up to 300 times, thereby creating more chances of hurting the back.

I have been placing a lot of emphasis on the sleeping posture right from the beginning, and I am mentioning it again.

While the preferred sleeping position is on the stomach, it may not suit everyone. Try sleeping on your back or side with your knees slightly bent with a comfortable pillow placed between the knees. This avoids exerting the back.

- Ensure that the mattress is firm enough to support the curvature of your spine.

- Don't get up from your bed with a jerk. Take your time, stretch a little in the bed if you can, then slowly turn over to one side, and get up by using the elbow of one arm, and the palm of the other hand for support.

- A towel roll should be placed below the lower back, and one pillow below the knees while lying on your back.

7

KNEE, FOOT AND SHOULDER PAIN

Weight will put more strain on your knees. Weight management is very important to prevent not only pain, but also RSI.

Small Tips for the Knee Pain Prevention

- Periodical weight check-up: Putting on weight will put more strain on your knees. Weight management is very important to prevent not only knee pain, but also RSI.

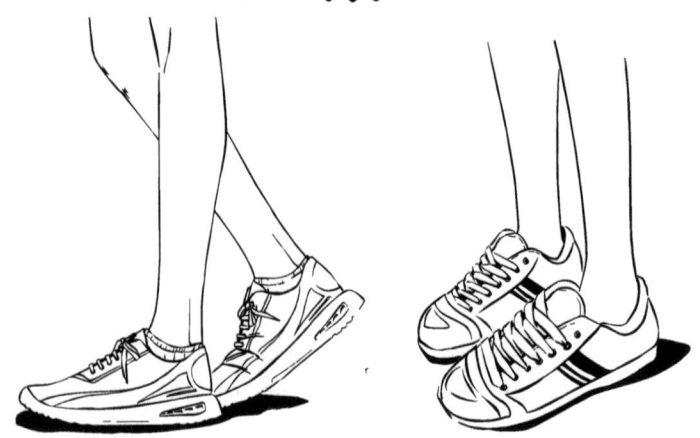

- Switch to sports shoes to reduce twisting stresses on the knees.
- Do weight shifts while standing in the kitchen by using a small step.
- Keep one foot on the step, and exchange the foot after 5 minutes. This will prevent placing excessive pressure on both the knees.

Avoiding any Kind of Knee Pain

- Avoid sitting with the legs crossed.
- Avoid prolonged duration of activities, which strain the joints (gardening, prolonged standing, kneeling and squatting, etc.).
- Avoid jerky movements.

- Avoid stairs. Climbing stairs puts immense pressure on the knees. It should be avoided at any cost. If your house has stairs, plan your day in such a way that you climb the stairs only once.
- Avoid a treadmill. Walking on a soft surface is more beneficial, compared to running on a hard surface (treadmill) because of the pressure placed on the ligaments and menisci (knee cushions).This can lead to early degenerative changes in the knee joint.
- Letting your legs hang while sitting should be avoided, as this causes oedema or swelling in the feet. Keep a foot stool in front of your leg and keep it elevated.
- Avoid sitting for long durations. Take breaks, walk for some time (5-10 min).

Pain Prevention

I have already mentioned the importance of soft soles and the correct footwear.

- Wear footwear with soft and cushioned soles.
- Avoid flat shoes and high-heels, as both adversely affect your feet, knees and back.

- Ensure that your shoes are of the right size. There should be a gap of the width of a thumb between your big toe and the end of the shoe. Keep your back straight and maintain a good posture while walking or standing.
- After a day of exertion, if your feet ache, take a warm water bath for 5-10 min.

Small Tips for Shoulder Pain Prevention

- Exercise regularly to maintain strength, flexibility and range of motion. Always keep the affected arm supported.
- Don't sleep on the affected side to avoid putting pressure, which can lead to more pain.
- Don't lift heavy weights with the affected arm.
- Don't jerk your shoulder. This will avoid unnecessary stress.
- Don't use the arm to push yourself up in bed or from a chair, because this requires a forceful contraction of muscles.
- Don't participate in contact sports, or repetitive heavy lifting.

8
ARTHRITIS

Arthritis means inflammation of one or more joints. It is a disease that causes painful inflammation and stiffness of the joints. It usually refers to joint pain or joint disease. It is a very common disease which can affect people of all ages, sexes and races and it is a leading cause of disability. It can also cause permanent joint changes in a person's body.

There are millions of adults and about 3,00,000 children who suffer from some type of arthritis. It is very common among women, and occurs more frequently in comparison with males when they get older.

This continuous weight for many years over the joint, is what causes the cartilage to breakdown, which then damages the joints. Therefore, people with excess weight are at greater risk of developing osteoarthritis, as compared to others.

(ii) *Genes:* The genetic traits of a person can also expose him/her to the risk of developing osteoarthritis. So, people with genetic osteoarthritis are affected as early as 20 years of age, which in turn makes the wear and tear faster than usual.

(iii) *Injury:* Injury to joints like fracture, surgery or ligament tears, also lead to osteoarthritis.

People who repeatedly damage their joints, tendons, or ligaments, develop osteoarthritis.

(iv) *Overuse:* When joints are overused; be it prolonged standing, heavy lifting, or other similar movements, these can break down the cartilage faster, which leads to the development of osteoarthritis in joints.

There are some other factors as well, which are responsible for osteoarthritis, such as certain types of metabolic disorders, hemochromatosis, or rheumatoid arthritis, etc.

Treatments: Who can treat a person suffering from osteoarthritis?

> *Any person suffering from osteoarthritis should consult physiotherapist or occupational therapist.*

Physiotherapists usually ask patients to refrain from taking any painkillers, except in cases of extreme pain, because the main purpose is to treat the condition that causes this pain, and not the symptom. Painkillers have side effects and can damage the kidneys and/or the stomach. They are usually prescribed when the patient is in extreme pain.

Drug Treatments: The medicines available to treat osteoarthritis are usually pills, lotions, syrups or injections. There are many treatments available in Allopathy, Ayurveda, and Homopathy that can be availed to treat osteoarthritis.

Therapies: There are different types of therapies for pain management.

Physical and Occupational Therapy: Physical and occupational therapists can provide a range of different treatments for pain management:

- Ways to properly use joints
- Heat and cold therapies
- Motion and flexibility exercises
- Treatment with modalities

Surgery: The treatments provided to patients are intended to prevent surgery. In some extreme cases, surgery may be the only option.

> Surgery is usually kept as the last option by most physiotherapists.

A doctor will refer an eligible patient to an orthopaedic surgeon to perform the procedure.

> Apart from physical, drug or ayurvedic treatments, a positive attitude also helps boost the immunity of a person which in turn helps to prevent a surgery or make a treatment work effectively.

II. Rheumatoid Arthritis

A disease in which the joints in the body become inflamed is called 'rheumatoid arthritis'. It is an autoimmune disease. The body's immune system, instead of protecting the body by attacking foreign substances, starts attacking the joints. This creates thickening of the tissue that lines the inside of the joints, resulting in swelling, pain and inflammation of the joints.

It is also called 'asystemic disease' because it can also affect the cardiovascular and the respiratory system in a person's body.

Rheumatoid arthritis most commonly affects the joints of the hands, feet, wrists, elbows, knees and ankles. The effect is usually symmetrical, and if one side is affected, the other side also gets affected.

What happens in rheumatoid arthritis is that the membrane (synovial fluid), which surrounds the joint to provide lubrication to keep the cartilage slippery and help the joint move smoothly, gets inflamed, and as a result, the joint hurts.

Symptoms: Initially, no redness or swelling is seen by the patient, but pain may be experienced.

Some of the symptoms experienced in rheumatoid arthritis are the following:

- More than one joint is affected
- Small joints (wrists, certain joints of the hands and feet) are affected
- The same joints on both sides of the body are affected
- Joint pain, tenderness, swelling or stiffness for six weeks or longer
- Morning stiffness that lasts for 30 minutes or longer
- Mild to severe pain
- Fatigue
- Loss of appetite and a low-grade fever
- It can also affect organs like eyes, lungs, blood, etc.

Causes: There is no specific cause that has been discovered yet, but hormones, genes and environmental factors that add to obesity or related problems, are usually considered responsible for causing rheumatoid arthritis. It often runs in families.

According to experts, the treatment for rheumatoid arthritis should be started as early as possible if a person is suffering from pain, swelling in the joint, and stiffness in the morning. If rheumatoid arthritis is left unchecked, it might cause severe damage to the joints, which is then incurable if it reaches the last stage. It can also cause permanent change to the joints. So, if rheumatoid arthritis is to be managed effectively, it is very important to diagnose it as early as possible.

Work Induced Rheumatic Problems: If the physical working method of a person changes, this may sometimes cause a rheumatic problem. If the same part of the body keeps getting strained, then a person will be more prone to rheumatic problems, and the symptoms of rheumatoid arthritis will only get worse.

At work where people are overstressed, and have a prolonged sitting or standing period, are more susceptible to developing rheumatoid arthritis. Staying active helps in the prevention of this kind of disease.

Physiotherapists often provide rheumatic patients who suffer from knee pain or lower back pain with belts, which are positioned accordingly to prevent more strain to be taken by the body part/s.

As we are familiar with the symptoms of rheumatoid arthritis, there are some situations that cause this problem while working.

- Stressful work conditions
- Sudden change in the working condition of a person
- Changing conditions at work that put excess stress over an individual

Work induced rheumatic problems generally occur in the arms and shoulders. The common problems with arms and shoulders developed through constantly working in the wrong position are:

- ***Shoulder Problems:*** By working in a wrong position, a person can develop problems in his/her shoulders, and a result in his/her arms as well. For example, a frozen shoulder.

- **Carpal Tunnel Syndrome:** When the median nerve in the carpal tunnel on the underside of the nerve is compressed, then carpal tunnel syndrome can occur.
- **Epicondylitis:** It is a type of mild inflammation of the location where the forearm muscles are joined to the bones of the elbow. The repetitive movements put continuous strain on the forearm muscles and cause epicondylitis.
- Work stress can also cause rheumatic problems to the lower back and knees.

A person, who is affected with rheumatic problems caused due to work, may experience the following symptoms:

- Warm feeling or burning
- Pins and needles being felt in hands or other area
- Weakness
- Pain
- Clumsiness
- Cramps

A patient who is suffering from problems due to work stress is advised to take anti-inflammatory medicines, and see a rheumatologist. They can recommend some lifestyle changes that a person can adopt to treat this condition successfully. Usually, a patient is asked to refrain from doing a task for more than 15 minutes, if his/her symptoms start affecting him/her during the repetitive activity.

The physical treatment also helps in treating this condition. The physiotherapists provide posture correction exercises to the patient which he/she can do on his/her own, or take physiotherapy sessions at a clinic. The heat and cold therapies are also very effective in treating the condition.

The recovery of a person varies, as individual conditions are considered in treating the problem. If a problem is treated in the early stages, it takes less time to recover and problems that take longer to develop, also take longer to recover.

III. Ankylosing Spondylitis

Ankylosing spondylitis is a type of arthritis that affects the spine. Ankylosing spondylitis symptoms include pain and stiffness from the neck, down to the lower back. The spine's bones (vertebrae) fuse together, resulting in a rigid spine. These changes may be mild or severe, and may lead to a stooped-over posture. Early diagnosis and treatment helps to control pain and stiffness, and may reduce or prevent significant deformity.

Symptoms: The most common early symptoms of ankylosing spondylitis include:

- ***Pain and Stiffness:*** Constant pain and stiffness in the lower back, buttocks and hips that continue for more than three months. Spondylitis often starts around the sacroiliac joints, where the sacrum (the lowest major part of the spine) joins the ilium bone of the pelvis in the lower back region.

- ***Bony Fusion:*** Ankylosing spondylitis can cause an overgrowth of the bones, which may lead to abnormal joining of bones, called 'bony fusion'. Fusion affecting bones of the neck, back or hips may impair a person's ability to perform routine activities. Fusion of the ribs to the spine or breastbone may limit a person's ability to expand his/her chest when taking a deep breath.

- *Pain in Ligaments and Tendons:* Spondylitis may also affect some of the ligaments and tendons that attach to bones. Tendonitis (inflammation of the tendon) may cause pain and stiffness in the area behind or beneath the heel, such as the Achilles tendon at the back of the ankle.

Causes: Although the cause of ankylosing spondylitis is unknown, there is a strong genetic or family link. Most people with spondylitis carry a gene called HLA-B27. Although people carrying this gene are more likely to develop spondylitis, it is also found in up to 10 per cent of people who have no signs of the condition.

Treatment: There is no cure for ankylosing spondylitis, but there are treatments that can reduce discomfort and improve function. The goals of treatment are to reduce pain and stiffness, maintain a good posture, prevent deformity and preserve the ability to perform normal activities. When properly treated, people with ankylosing spondylitis may lead normal lives. Under ideal circumstances, a team approach to treat spondylitis is recommended. Members of the treatment team typically include the patient, doctor, physical therapist, and occupational therapist. In patients with severe deformities, osteotomy and fusion can be done.

- ***Physical and Occupational Therapy:*** Early intervention with physical and occupational therapy is important to maintain function and minimize deformity.

- ***Exercise:*** A programme of daily exercise helps reduce stiffness, strengthen the muscles around the joints and prevent or minimize the risk of disability. Deep breathing exercises may help keep the chest cage flexible. Swimming is an excellent form of exercise for people with ankylosing spondylitis.

- ***Medications:*** Certain drugs help provide relief from pain and stiffness, and allow patients to perform their exercises with minimal discomfort.

- ***Surgery:*** Artificial joint replacement surgery may be a treatment option for some people with advanced joint disease affecting the hips or knees.

IV. Psoriatic Arthritis

Psoriatic arthritis is a form of inflammatory arthritis that can affect people who have psoriasis. Psoriasis is a skin disease that causes a red, scaly rash, most commonly over the elbows, knees, ankles, feet, hands and other areas.

Symptoms: Symptoms include pain and swelling in the hands, wrists, elbows, shoulders, knees, ankles, feet and spine; morning stiffness, and fatigue like that of rheumatoid arthritis (inflammatory arthritis). Psoriatic arthritis can also cause inflammation in other areas of the body, including the eyes.

Treatment: Treatment for psoriatic arthritis consists of twice daily moist heat or cold applications, exercises, and non-steroidal anti-inflammatory drugs. If there is little improvement, or if there are permanent changes visible on an x-ray, then a disease modifying antirheumatic drug or a biologic drug will be added, to help prevent long-term joint damage. Enzyme inhibitors such as apremilast (Otezla) can also be prescribed to block proteins that cause the inflammation.

Factors Causing Pain in the Back

Sprains and Strains: Back pain is also caused by everyday activities that put stress on backs. But in such injuries which are mostly ignored, the body heals itself by trying to splint the painful area which creates cramps. This causes weakness to the muscle and once it is weak, it may cause any type of problem.

Spinal Stenosis: When the back pain is associated with the pain in the legs while walking, it is known as 'spinal stenosis'. In this condition, the nerve or the spinal cord is compressed due to the thickening of any of the main spinal ligament.

Spondylosis: The back pain that occurs due to arthritis of facet joints, and degeneration of the disc is called 'spondylosis'. It often affects the lower back and the neck. Pain is not a necessary symptom in this condition. It may be accompanied with severe pain or with no pain at all.

Other Causes: Other causes which may be responsible for back pain are:

- Trauma or any physical injury

- Infection
- Tumour
- Inflammation
- Fracture often due to the thinning of bones known as 'osteoporosis'.

Exercises

There are various exercises provided by the therapists to treat the condition or to prevent back pain. If the muscles are strong, then work related problems don't cause issues, and a person stays healthy in a work stressed environment as well. But if the muscles are weak, it is very easy to develop problems with the joint, muscle or ligaments.

A person should stay healthy by staying flexible with exercises, and building his or her stamina. But these exercises are to be done very carefully, and if done in excess, or not in a prescribed way, can make the condition worse or even create one.

The following are the exercises recommended by the physiotherapists to prevent or treat the conditions of back pain:

Stretching Exercises

Step 1

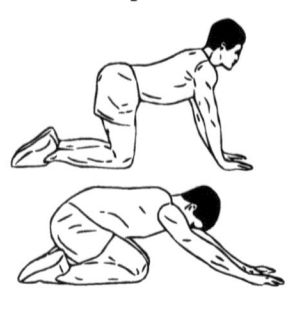

bottom to heels stretch

Step 2

opposite arm/leg raises

Step 3

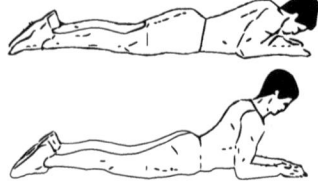

back extensions

Step 4

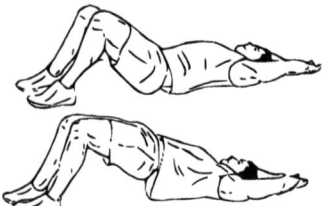

bridges

Step 5

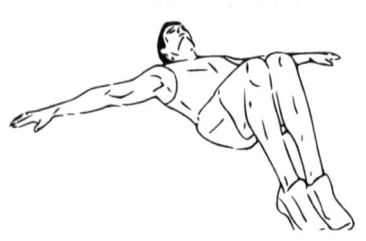

Knee rolls

Stamina-building Exercises

Any exercise recommended by physiotherapists should be done in the prescribed way, as in how much to do, when to do it, and how to do it.

> *Every individual's body is different; therefore, what will suit one person may not suit another. So, it is important to talk to your physiotherapist before starting these exercises.*

Refraining (Cautions)

In order to ensure that the back pain doesn't get worse, a patient is advised not to do the following things:

- Not exercising regularly
- Prolonged standing
- Prolonged sitting in one position only
- Heavy weightlifting
- Bending too much
- Stress

There are some ergonomically designed corsets which are customised according to the patient's requirement which also help in treating back pain. But, it is better to strengthen muscles, so that patients don't depend on corsets only.

Manipulations also help in treating back pain. There are different types of manipulations and they vary according to the patients.

Many patients consider changing their bed, as they believe that this may be the cause. Not sleeping well, and having a too hard or too soft a mattress, can cause pain in the body, which adds to this problem. The beds should be neither too hard nor too soft, but as required by every patient; according to their bodies, and problems that they are suffering from.

Diet Modification and Arthritis

A change in diet can certainly help a person overcome the problem of arthritis.

- A person should have a balanced and nutritious meal which can provide his/her body with vitamins, minerals, antioxidants and other nutrients to keep him/her healthy which includes consuming plenty of vegetables and fruits.

- The oil and fat consumption should be controlled.
- A regular exercise routine helps the body in using these nutrients effectively, keeping the body in a healthy state.
- Fish oil helps in protection against heart disease, and is good for health as well.
- Weight monitoring is very important in terms of preventing arthritis, as being overweight can cause stress over the back, knees and the ankles. This constant struggle between the body parts and the excess weight of the body makes the joints weaker and more prone to arthritis. Patients are advised to cut down on fatty and sugary foods to prevent arthritis, which result from excess weight. Therefore, weight management is very important if a person wants to prevent arthritis.

There are many treatments available, which can help in losing weight, but some of them are usually not permanent, and hence the weight returns. So, it is better to stick to a healthy diet which helps a person stay fit, and has no other side effects.

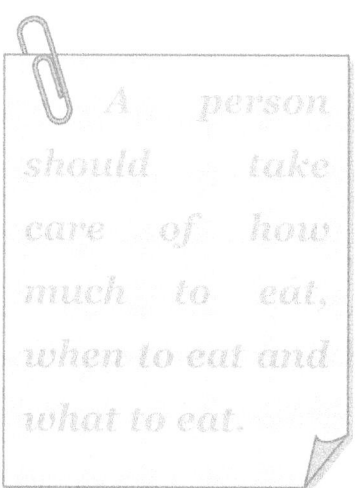

A person should take care of how much to eat, when to eat and what to eat.

These are very important in preventing arthritis, as quantity and quality of food affect health the most. Some preventive steps to remain fit and avoid obesity are:

- Choosing lean cuts of meat
- Consuming fish and poultry
- Consuming Low fat oils
- Avoiding fried food
- Eating plenty of fruits and vegetables

- Taking snacks which are low in fat
- Using low fat dairy products
- Avoiding fat-rich snacks, like biscuits, chocolates, etc.
- Eating salads more often
- Taking plenty of water and juices
- Fasting can prove beneficial in rheumatoid arthritis, but it can also return after the person returns to his/her normal diet. Therefore, fasting should be done under the supervision of a specialist.

A vegan diet helps in this type of arthritis, but because it is difficult to get all the nutrients from a vegan diet, supplements should be added as well.

Food Allergies

Certain food allergies may increase the problem. Therefore, it is important to test for food allergies.

People suffering from gout often cut down on oranges, grapefruit, or other fruits believing that it might be helpful, however there is no scientific evidence that avoiding these foods can be helpful in relieving this problem. So, diet should be chosen carefully, and for providing the body with all the required nutrients. One should maintain a balanced diet, which will keep the body in a healthy state.

Skimmed milk has more calcium than the fatty milk that we usually drink. Therefore, fat should be cut down, but nutrients should be kept in balance, because if the body lacks these essential nutrients, it becomes difficult to recover and stay fit.

9

PREVENTION DURING PREGNANCY

Pregnancy is the most beautiful phase of a woman's life. As a woman needs to carry a new life within her, she needs to take additional care of herself, but it does not mean that she should not work during pregnancy. Some people believe that a pregnant lady should not work, and should rest all the time, but this is a myth. In fact, an active lifestyle is much more beneficial, as compared to a sedentary one.

I would like to discuss the topic of prevention during pregnancy. Antenatal care, which means 'care during pregnancy', is very important. Small precautions taken during pregnancy can prevent post-delivery problems like back pain, neck pain, weight gain, etc. Antenatal care is a very vast topic, but I want to mention that the traditional thoughts or beliefs about pregnancy should be overcome by knowledge and awareness. There is no need to keep eating and sleeping during pregnancy. Pregnancy is not a problem; it is a beautiful phase of life which nature has blessed us with.

Additional calorie consumption of ~300 calories during pregnancy is important. Frequent and small meals are also important. During the early stages of pregnancy, one should eat a healthy and balanced diet, instead of a fat-rich diet. It is very easy to digest, and helps to avoid nausea, vomiting, acidity, breathlessness, etc.

A pregnant woman should do antenatal and postnatal exercises to avoid common problems faced during pregnancy. There are so many changes which take place during pregnancy, and some of these changes can cause irritation and discomfort. Some common problems during pregnancy are backache, constipation cramps, deep vein thrombosis (DVT), faintness, hot flashes, headaches, indigestion, heartburn, itching, morning sickness and nausea, frequent urination, pelvic pain, sleeplessness, stretch marks, swollen ankles, feet, fingers, tiredness, varicose veins, etc.

To avoid many of these problems, we need to do some basic exercises which include:

- Pelvic floor muscle training
- Core stability training
- Exercises for strength
- Exercises for flexibility
- Balance exercises
- Postural awareness is required. Doctors recommend sleeping on the left side as it increases the blood flow to the uterus and placenta.
- Upper limb strengthening exercises to help carry the baby after birth.
- Breathing exercises
- Stretching exercises

Doing these simple exercises and maintaining proper hygiene can lead to a healthy pregnancy. Even after delivery, postnatal care to reduce weight and maintain physique is important to return to normal life once again.

PREVENTION DURING PREGNANCY

Regular, gentle exercise in pregnancy, particularly ankle and leg movements, will improve your circulation and may help to prevent cramps.

Try the following foot exercises:

- Bend and stretch your foot vigorously up and down thirty times.

- Rotate your foot eight times one way and eight times the other way.

- Repeat with the other foot.

It is the duty of a physiotherapist to properly assess, treat and educate pregnant women in effective and safe exercises that have been shown to decrease back pain, pelvic pain and urinary incontinence—throughout their pregnancy and post-partum.

10

ROLE OF DIET

Diet plays a vital role in healthy living and prevention of several diseases and physical problems related to bones/joints. Maintaining a healthy weight, according to your age, can prevent not only the bone-joint problems, but also medical conditions like high-blood pressure and diabetes; incidence of which has increased drastically due to poor lifestyle. **Being overweight or underweight also causes higher risk of RSI.**

If you are trying to lose excess weight, the combination of a healthy diet and exercise is the key to success. When you exercise regularly, you may experience an increased appetite. Knowing how to fuel your body with healthy options can help keep you satisfied, and cause weight loss.

Diet helps bridge the gap as your body stabilizes itself in response to regular exercise. Over time, workouts may become less effective. Putting exercise and diet together will improve your health from inside out. Physical activity reduces your risk of heart disease, cancer, obesity and diabetes. Good nutrition improves your heart health, brain health and energy levels, and helps control your weight. Both can also improve your immune system, boost your mood and help you sleep better. In truth, neither diet nor exercise alone will help you achieve your weight loss goals. If you want to maintain optimum health, a healthy diet and regular exercise routine must be done concurrently.

An appropriate dietary management strategy should begin with a basic understanding of the interrelationship between calories ingested and expended. The critical balance between energy intake and energy expenditure determines body weight. The goal is to manipulate lifestyle through eating and exercise so that the obese individual's energy balance is negative over 24 hours. This means he or she has expended more calories than ingested. This can be achieved by: (1) decreasing food intake and keeping physical activity constant; (2) keeping food intake constant and increasing physical activity; or (3) decreasing food intake and increasing physical activity simultaneously.

In the past, most emphasis was placed on the first option. That is, the number of calories ingested formed the focal point of weight loss programs. Total fasts, in which less than 200 calories were ingested in 24 hours, had been used for quick weight loss. This type of program was harmful to the individual's lean body mass, which was consumed along with fat to maintain life. The current consensus among nutrition scientists is that a balanced low-fat diet, in combination with regular physical activity, is the recommended approach to weight loss and maintenance. The given table summarizes the main characteristics of an appropriate and healthy dietary intake.

Healthy weight also gives us confidence and freedom to wear any clothing in style. By healthy weight, I don't mean you should go on a crash diet to become size zero!

Total Calories	**Women:** no less than 1200 calories/day **Men:** no less than 1500 calories/day
Fat	30% of calories or less, reducing levels of saturated and trans fatty acids
Protein	20% to 25% of calories, averaging no less than 75 g/day
Carbohydrates	50% of calories, no less than 5 servings of fruits and vegetables daily Minimizing the ingestion of processed simple (table sugar) and complex (starches) sugars
Dietary Fiber	20-30 g/day from food sources
Water	Drink at least 2 to 3 liters of water per day
Alcohol	Limited or none

Being underweight can present as many health concerns to an individual as being overweight can. If a person is underweight, their body may not be getting the nutrients it needs to build healthy bones, skin, and hair. Using the BMI is considered a good measure of a person's weight because it compares their weight to their height. For example, a 170-pound person may not be overweight if they are very tall but could be overweight if they are very short.

Ranges for BMI include:

- **Underweight:** less than 18.5
- **Normal/healthy weight:** 18.5 to 24.9
- **Overweight:** 25.0 to 29.9
- **Obese:** 30 or higher

These calculations may be slightly inaccurate for a person who is an elite or endurance athlete whose body has a significant amount of muscle. This is because muscle weighs more than fat.

If a person is underweight, there are various healthful weight-gain methods that they can try. A person can gain weight by following a healthful diet that incorporates nutritious calorie-dense foods. A dietician can help a person develop a diet plan that works for them.

Some key components of a diet for weight gain may include:

- **Adding snacks:** High-protein and whole-grain carbohydrate snacks can help a person gain weight. Examples include peanut butter crackers, protein bars, trail mix, pita chips and hummus, or a handful of almonds.

- **Eating several small meals a day:** Sometimes a person may be underweight because they cannot tolerate eating large meals. Instead, a person can eat several small meals throughout the day.

- **Incorporating additional foods:** A person can add calorie-dense food sources to their existing diet, such as putting slivered almonds on top of cereal or yogurt, sunflower or chia seeds on a salad or soup, or nut butter on whole-grain toast.

- **Avoiding empty calories:** Eating high-calorie foods may cause a person to gain weight, but they also have excess fats that could affect a person's heart and blood vessels. A person should avoid foods that are high in sugar and salt.

After a good workout, good diet is very important.

1. Your day should start with healthy breakfast followed by moderate lunch and a light and early dinner. Try to have dinner before 7 pm.

2. Avoid junk food, processed food and meals high in saturated fat.

ROLE OF DIET

3. Drink two to three liters of water a day to flush out any toxins in the body.

4. If you have any doubts, get a diet plan made for yourself by a dietician or nutritionist.

11
LIFESTYLE MODIFICATIONS

Lifestyle modifications are simple alterations in long term eating and physical activity habits. It can help to manage a range of diseases.

Lifestyle modifications should begin from childhood.

Modifications for Children

- When a child is young, the way he/she carries the school bag should be corrected.

- Kids in school have heavy bags. They carry the bag on one shoulder. They sit in wrong postures, which leads to muscle spasms. If not corrected at the right age, it can lead to RSI.

- A conscious effort should be made to maintain the right posture, carry the school bag on both shoulders (backpack), carry light weight school bags and wear soft sole shoes.

- A proper study table with a light lamp focused on the book should be provided to the child. Too bright of a light can also strain a child's eyes.

Modifications for Adults

- Don't stand for long periods; keep shifting weight from one leg to another.

- Take your shoes off, and wiggle your toes to enable circulation of blood.

- Don't wear high heeled uncomfortable shoes. The best shoes for your feet and back are the ones that are cushioned and flat.

Modifications for Tall People

- You must walk straight and maintain a correct posture. We have seen in many especially in tall people, that they tend to bend forward while walking. Incorrect posture during walking shifts the line of gravity away from neutral, putting more stress on joints and muscles, thereby causing body pain.

Modifications while Driving a Car

- Adjust the driving seat so that your knee is not touching the dashboard. The back of the seat should be straight, so that while driving you are sitting straight, and your back is always supported.

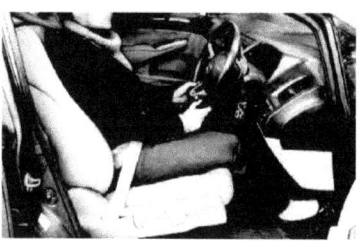

- While driving car, do not hold on to the gear as your hand will remain unsupported for a long time, and you may experience pain in the shoulder and neck. After changing the gear, put your hand to its original position, or rest your hand on your thigh (left hand).

- Don't hold the steering wheel too tight, keeping both elbows straight, as that puts unnecessary strain on the shoulder and neck.

- Hold the steering wheel low so that your elbows are bent.

- Sit reclined with your shoulders bent slightly.

- Sit back from the steering wheel as far as possible while remaining in safe control of the vehicle.

- Hold the outside rim of the steering wheel slightly lowered down. This position will minimize the risk of injury to your arms, hands and fingers in an accident, when airbag deploys.

- Arms should be bent slightly.

- You should be able to pivot your right foot from the accelerator to the brake pedal without lifting your heel from the floor.
- Don't talk on the mobile phone while driving.
- Avoid rash driving, as it increases stress and constricts body movement, which is not good.

12

GOOD POSTURE GOODIES

Good posture is one of the most fundamental elements of maintaining good health, well-being and being free of pain. The question arises: what is good posture, and why is it so important? Basically, posture refers to the body's alignment and positioning with respect to the ever-present force of gravity. Whether we are standing, sitting or lying down, gravity exerts a force on our joints, ligaments and muscles. Good posture entails distributing this force of gravity through our body so that no any structure is overstressed.

It is difficult to maintain good posture if the overall body mechanism is not under perfect control. The position of individual body parts is of crucial importance in order to achieve a good posture. Practising a good posture is the key to preventing long-term injuries.

Our muscles hold our joints in alignment, so that they may move efficiently and effectively, however, when the posture is not what it should be, muscles contract, weaken and the joints may move out of alignment. If an imperfect posture becomes a habit, it can lead to knee, shoulder and hip issues. It is more important to learn about the causes (improper postural alignment), than to treat the pain, which is nothing other than a symptom. One of the things that helps people look and feel better, is their own 'posture'.

> *Good posture is the correct alignment through body parts that are needed to maintain balance and stability with less effort and least strain during supportive and non-supportive positions.*

The right knowledge of postural alignments will help in the assessment of the related postural problem areas. A study published in the International Journal of Scientific and Technology Research (2013) that tracked 400 IT professionals in India stated that 51% of the participants reported lower back pain and that this was the number one musculoskeletal disorder of employees in IT industry.

> *Good posture increases energy and stamina. When your ribcage is in the correct position, you can inhale more air. The more oxygen you breathe, the more energy you get.*

Correct body posture reduces chances of neck and back pain. The more aligned the spine is, lower is the strain on the neck and back muscles. Unless the pain is caused by some sort of impact injury, we know that damaged soft tissues are a result of poor posture.

> *Postural-alignment exercise can improve other joint-related alignments of the knees, hips and ankles. When the pelvis is in the incorrect position, certain muscles don't work well, thereby placing undue stress on the lower limb joints.*

We must listen to our body symptoms when we feel pain anytime and anywhere in our body.

Back Pain Progresses with Age

At earlier stage of life, things are usually in place. For example, a child does not need to drive a car, bend over a phone or stand hunched for hours. Children spend most of their time in playing, jumping, lifting things and sleeping. So, there is no chance of postural misalignment in children. But, as we grow, it starts creeping up and taking a toll over our overall health. The chronic misalignments get worse over time from years of repetitive actions.

> *If you know and practice the correct posture, you will be able to reduce your chances of carpel tunnel symptoms like pain in hands and fingers that can arise as a result of excessive texting and computer work. When the cervical spine (neck area) is out of alignment, it can leave negative impact on shoulders, elbows and wrists. When the tendons in the wrist get strained, pain can radiate to the hands.*

Human body is more complex than a simple set of building blocks. The joints are supposed to be held together by the muscles. However, when the muscles get tight, weak or overused, the joints move further and further out of alignment, the result being poor posture.

The picture at the right illustrates the proper standing posture. You can see a straight line drawn through the middle of the body, starting from the ear, moving down into the shoulder, through the hips, the centre of the knee joint, and just in front of the ankle bones. This is called the 'plumb line'. Our goal is to get this proper alignment and most people have some sort of misalignment that deviates from this ideal alignment.

Tips to Maintain Good Standing Posture

- Bear the weight on your feet.
- Keep your knees slightly bent.
- Keep your feet about shoulder-width.
- Keep your hands in your pockets.
- Stand straight and tall with your shoulders pulled backward.

- Tuck your stomach in.
- Keep your head level. Your earlobes should be in line with your shoulders and don't push your head forward, backward, or to the side.
- Shift your weight from toes to heels or one foot to the other (if you must stand for a long time).

Now, we will discuss two major postural deviations that are seen in most of the population. We will describe what happens most often with the upper body – hunchback – and the lower half – arched back.

Upper-body Postural Deviations
Hunchback Posture (Kyphosis)

It is estimated that today at least 90% of the population is suffering from this ailment. Unless you regularly engage in alignment-focused workouts, like Yoga, etc., the chances are there that you have a hunchback posture.

Hunchback-posture muscle features include:

- Tight pectoral (chest) muscles
- Tight latissimus dorsi (sides of the back) muscles

- Tight upper trapezius (neck) muscles
- Weak erector spinae (around the spine) muscles
- Weak mid/lower trapezius (mid back) muscles
- Weak deep cervical spine (neck) muscles
- Weak posterior deltoid (back of shoulders) muscles

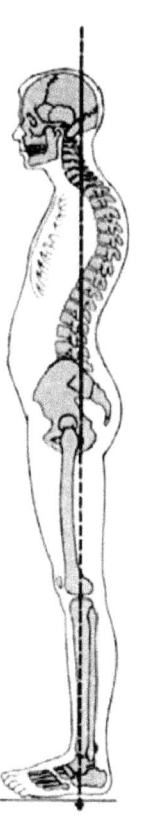

You will notice this posture among the people with desk jobs, in the older population, in women with larger bust sizes, in teenagers who are glued to their cell phones, and finally those who do not pay attention to it.

Have you ever wondered why your neck hurts by just sitting at your desk for a while, and why neck massages only help for a few hours and, eventually, the pain returns? This comes from the constant pressure of the 'bowling ball' leaning forward in a position that is unnatural and unintended. The building blocks are off course, and the muscles around it were not meant to handle this load.

This particular issue has exacerbated over the years due to our advancement in technology, which require us to sit facing forward, with our hands below our chest on a keyboard, and our eyes looking forward and down towards a screen. Things have turned even worse as the popularity of texting and cell phones has risen. What do we do all day? We look down, we lean forward, we round our shoulders and we hunch.

Assessment

- Stand up against a wall with your heels two inches in front of the wall.
- Your butt will be against the wall but your lower back will not touch the wall.
- Push your head up against the wall with your chin parallel to the floor.
- Make sure your front ribs are not sticking out and jutting forward.

Pull your ribs into your spine.

- Are you able to feel the back of your shoulders against the wall? If not, you have a hunchback posture.
- If you feel your shoulders against the wall, does doing so require you to stick your ribs out and work hard? If so, you have a hunchback posture.

> *The hunchback is a chronic postural problem that gets worse every year, especially for the younger and more technology-savvy generations.*

Lower-Body Postural Deviations

Arched-Back Posture (Lumbar-Lordosis): Lordosis (arched back) is a very common problem and commonly occurs in conjunction with kyphosis (hunchback). This posture is often seen in people who sit at a desk or at a computer all day long. The lower back arches excessively, causing a deeper 'C' shape of the lumbar spine. If you examine this posture, you can see how excessive jumping, lifting, running or even stretching, with the back in this position, can put pressure on the vertebra in the lumbar spine, causing compression, disc issue and lower back pain.

Arched-back posture muscle features include:

- Tight hip flexor (front of the hips) muscles
- Tight erector spinae (sides of the spine) muscles
- Tight latissimus dorsi (sides of the back) muscles
- Weak deep intrinsic abdominal (stomach) muscles
- Weak gluteus medius and maximus (butt) muscles

The goal of any exercise routine for someone with this posture is to bring the pelvis back into a neutral position, where there is more of a natural 'C' shape in the spine. This means finding exercises that emphasize stretching the hip flexors, strengthening the glutes and deepening the strength of the all-important abdominals. The core strengthening components of a regular Pilates practice can assist in correcting this postural misalignment.

Assessment:

- Stand normally and place hands in a triangle position with your fingers and thumbs touching.
- Place this triangle on your stomach area, with your fingertips touching your pubic bone and your thumbs below your belly button.
- Look down at your hands. Are your thumbs protruding forward more than your fingers? If so, then the top of your pelvis leans forward more, which means you have an arched-back posture.

Effects of Good Posture

- Makes different body functions and systems flawless.
- Helps in making the muscles relaxed and unloaded.
- Improves respiratory and circulatory efficiency.
- Prevents unnecessary strain and fatigue.
- Decreases the incidence of diseases resulting from bad postures.
- Improves the person's state — mentally and/or psychologically.

13

EASY TIPS AND TRICKS TO REMEMBER

Prevention is the key to leading a pain-free life. It is rightly said that 'prevention is worth a pound of painkillers'. In the following paragraphs, we will discuss prevention tips related to several body problems.

Arthritis

If you want to prevent arthritis, control your weight, exercise daily, control the uric acid level, and enjoy every moment of your life.

Tips to Prevent Arthritis

By following healthy habits, you can reduce the risk of Arthritis. Some of them are covered below:

- Control and maintain a healthy body weight.
- Avoid sitting cross legged and squatting.
- Don't smoke, or quit smoking. It reduces the chance of developing arthritis.
- Avoid using the treadmill while exercising to avoid osteoarthritis.
- Avoid prolonged duration of activities, which strain the joints (e.g. gardening, prolonged standing, kneeling and squatting, etc.).
- In order to get aerobic exercise, try playing tennis. You may also dance or walk, to get aerobic exposure.

Back Pain

If you want to say 'no' to back pain, or prevent its progression, regular exercise to keep your back healthy and strong is very important. In order to protect your back, learn how to lift objects safely. Along with it, be mindful of your posture, whether you are sitting or standing.

Wear low-heeled shoes and maintain a healthy weight to avoid excess strain on your lower back. Eat a healthy diet, manage stress and most importantly, if you smoke, quit the habit.

Tips to Prevent Back Pain

- Keep a rolled towel under your lower back while exercising lying down and sleeping.
- Wear soft or cushion sole footwear.
- Avoid flat shoes or high heels, and wear jogging shoes instead.
- Walk straight in a correct posture.
- Sit with your back straight with a well-supported pillow, especially while sitting in the car, working and travelling on a plane.
- While driving for a long period, try to take pit stops as often as possible.

- Don't slouch, as this will make your back curl and exert your lower back.

- While lifting any object, stand as close to the object as possible; bend only at the knees and keep your back straight. 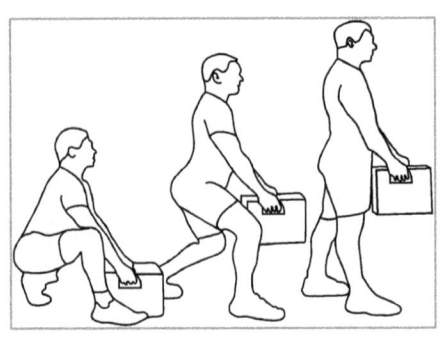 Secure your grip on the thing and lift it by straightening your knees.

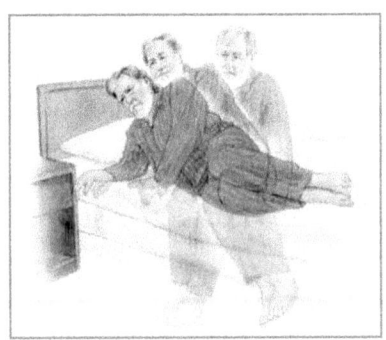

- Don't get up from your bed with a jerk. Take your time, stretch a little in the bed then slowly turn over to the side and get up by using the elbow of one arm and the palm of the other hand for support.

- Don't bend directly to tie shoe laces. Sit on a chair and keep the feet on a foot stool, and then tie your shoe laces.

Wear Soft Sole shoes on a Regular Basis, and minimize the use of heeled shoes

There is a connection between stiffness of the sole and health. In fact, the softness or stiffness of the sole that you wear does have a colossal effect on your health. If you are among those shoe-lovers who love to make their feet heavy, be cautious. Change your habits. Say 'no' to the heavy sole and embrace the soft sole.

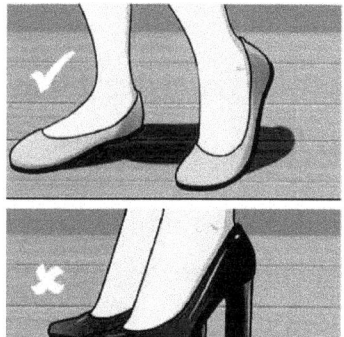

Support the Elbows while Working on a Computer

In the Digital world that we live in today, people spend most of their time in front of their computers, or on their mobile devices. Twitching of elbows is a common discomfort amongst computer users. The term 'twitching' is defined as the involuntary contractions of groups of muscle fibers. If you are among those whose elbows twitch, and stop randomly for a short period of time, it can be indicative of muscle cramps, nerve diseases or metabolism disturbances.

Avoid Carrying Heavy Luggage on Shoulders to Prevent Injuries

People commonly carry laptop bags or side use bags, and this creates an imbalance of the shoulder and neck muscles. Therefore, to maintain the equilibrium of your muscles, avoid lifting weights on one side. Either use a backpack or a trolley bag.

Early Detection of Deformities

Deformity can be dangerous if not recognised at an early stage. If left untreated, it can wreak havoc to the well-being of a person, and may be too late to reverse the damage. Therefore, the crucial point is not to ignore even a minor deformity, and bring it to the notice of the doctor at the earliest possible time.

Don't Ignore Body Signals – Early Attention Prevents Progression of Disease

There are certain kinds of body signals, you can ill afford to avoid. These body signals may indicate some serious problems that need immediate medical attention, and should be treated as early as possible.

Here it is important to note that pain is actually a defense mechanism. The system of our body uses it to get our attention, and it is the indication that something is not right. So, we should pay attention to it as early as possible.

Listed below are the some of the pain signals you should give immediate attention to:

- **Chest Pain:** Chest pain along with tachycardia (shortness of breath), could be a pre-heart attack symptom.

- **Joint Pain:** Joint pain can be anything, but normal. If you notice inflammation and redness in your joint, it may be a sign of rheumatoid arthritis.

- **Severe Headache:** Headaches are the least-cared of pains, regardless of their severity. Whenever anyone gets a headache he/she takes a pill and throws all the caution to the wind. But, we need to be utterly careful about the headaches. Headache can be a symptom of cerebral aneurysm.

Exercise Daily

You can choose an exercise based on your needs and requirements. Some of them are given below:

- **Chin Tuck:** This exercise strengthens the neck muscles and can be done sitting or standing. Start with your shoulders rolled back and down. While looking straight ahead, place two fingers on your chin, slightly tuck your chin and move your head back. Hold for a while and then release.

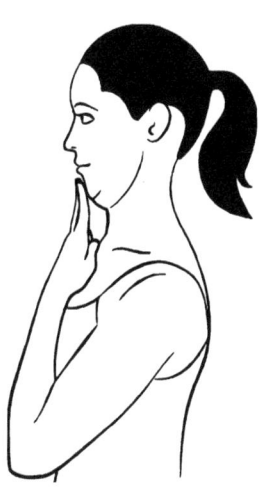

- **Wall Angel:** Stand with your back against a wall with your feet about four inches from the base. Maintain a slight bend in your knees. Your glutes, spine and head should all be against the wall. Bring your arms up with elbows bent so that your upper arms are parallel to the floor and squeeze your shoulder blades together, forming the letter 'W'. Hold for a while. Next, straighten your elbows to raise your arms up to form the letter

'Y'. Make sure not to shrug your shoulders to your ears.

- **Doorway Stretch:** This exercise strengthens the chest muscles. Standing in a doorway, lift your arm so that it's parallel to the floor and bend at the elbow so that your fingers point towards the ceiling. Place your hand on the doorjamb. Slowly lean into your raised arm and push against the doorjamb. Relax the pressure and then press your arm against the doorjamb again, this time coming into a slight lunge with your legs so that your chest moves forward past the doorjamb.

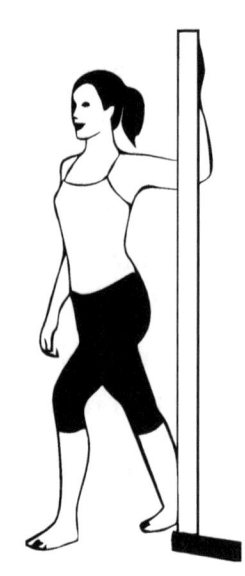

- **Hip Flexor Stretch:** Kneel onto your right knee with toes down, and place your left foot flat on the floor in front of you. Place both hands on your left thigh and press your hips forward

until you feel a good stretch in the hip flexors. Contract your abdominals and slightly tilt your pelvis back while keeping your chin parallel to the floor. Hold this pose for a little longer and then switch sides.

Consult your Physiotherapist before Starting Exercises

There are many people who can help you to maintain good health. So, to start and build your exercise routine, consult a physiotherapist if you have any physical problems. A physiotherapist will help you formulate an individualized exercise routine, based on your needs and help you stick to it. This will result in less pain and injury, a stronger body and mind, and increased flexibility.

When your physiotherapist designs an exercise plan for you, he/she will ensure that it fits in well with your unique fitness goals, lifestyle requirements, and is sustainable over a long period of time.

Exercise is Important for People with Arthritis

Exercise is important for people with arthritis. It increases strength and flexibility, reduces joint pain and helps combat fatigue. Of course, when stiff and painful joints are already bogging you down, the thought of walking around the block or swimming a few laps might seem overwhelming.

Eat Healthy

Healthy food allows your body to be healthy. So, let's go through the following list briefly on which foods to add to your diet:

- **4 tablespoons of olive oil:** consume about 4 tablespoons of olive oil per day. In a recent study, it showed that people, who had this measure of olive oil in their diet, decreased the risk of cardiovascular diseases.
- **400 grams of vegetables:** consume 400 grams of vegetables daily. Of that quantity, more than half should be raw, uncooked vegetables.
- **3 fruits:** consume more than 3 fruits per day.

- **450 grams legumes:** consume 450 grams of legumes per week.
- **350 grams fish:** consume 350 grams of fish per week.
- **White meat:** when one has a menu choice, always choose white meat over red meat.
- **Tomato-based sauces:** when looking at sauce choices, choose tomato-based sauces with added herbs, spices and garlic.

Physiotherapy is a must to Prevent Pain

Physiotherapist is the cornerstone of pain-related treatment. A physiotherapist can apply a variety of treatments, such as heat, ultrasound, electrical stimulation and muscle-release techniques to reduce pain. As the pain improves, the physiotherapist can teach you exercises that can increase your flexibility, strengthen your muscles and improve your posture. Regular use of these techniques can help to prevent pain from reoccurring.

14
Summary & Conclusion

We have covered a lot of ground in the previous chapters, and I hope that the topics covered will be helpful for my readers to lead a healthy and pain free life. I would like to summarize some of the key points that will be helpful reminders for everyone.

Repetitive Stress Injury:

- This is a frequent problem faced by many people, and is caused by repeating our basic tasks that make up our daily routine at home and at work.

- Awareness of the correct posture for various tasks, such as using a computer, or mobile phone etc. is extremely important.
- Neglecting the early signals can lead to structural disorders.

Posture:

- Correct posture is extremely important to avoid health issues.
- Familiarise yourself with the correct posture while sitting, standing, sleeping, walking, driving a car, etc.
- Remember the importance of choosing the right chair for sitting and shoes for walking.
- Focus on your own posture, but also be aware of your children's posture. Early corrections and reminders will lead to positive results in the long term.

Pain:

- Many of us will suffer from pain at some point in our lives.

- It is very important to listen to the pain signals that our body is transmitting and take the right steps to prevent long-term complications.

- Follow the tips on the Do's and Don'ts of the pains associated with the shoulder, neck, knee, back and foot.

Exercise:

- Moderate exercise can help you to maintain a healthy body weight and remain fit.

- Try low impact aerobic workouts like walking, swimming and cycling.

- While using a treadmill or cross trainer, limit the duration to 10 minutes each to avoid stress on the knees and hips. In case of any joint pain, avoid this form of exercise.

- Basic stretching and strengthening exercises will keep your joints and bones healthy.

- Do the proper warm-ups and cool down before and after exercises.

- Consult a physiotherapist who will design a tailored exercise program according to your personal health status. Self-selection of exercises may sometime harm you, if you have any underlying pathology that you are not aware of.

Diet:

- Maintaining a healthy weight is important and the combination of exercise and diet plays an important role in this regard.
- Diet plays a vital role in pain management. A person with chronic pain should avoid high glycemic food (simple carbohydrates), and eat more protein-rich food, fruits, and vegetables.
- Your day should start with a healthy breakfast, followed by a moderate lunch, and a light and early dinner.

This book is all about prevention. I hope I have explained the importance of prevention. I have already mentioned the list of Do's and Don'ts throughout the book which are important in daily life. Even if you don't remember what to do, you should never forget what not to do.

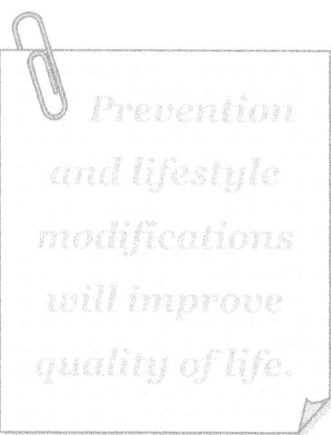

Prevention and lifestyle modifications will improve quality of life.

We always invest money in our future, fixed deposits, mutual funds, etc. thinking about a safe and secured future, but why don't we invest in our body today? To have a better quality of life and health in the future, you don't have to invest money, but just time.

Lightning Source UK Ltd.
Milton Keynes UK
UKHW021426300919
350728UK00013B/3156/P